THE STORY OF A SIREN:

The Beginning of the Sonic Warrior

A SIREN SAGA

JASON HUNTER

THE STORY OF A SIREN:

CONTENTS

1. TJ and Ashley — 1
2. Where Everything Breaks — 5
3. A New Day — 11
4. The Soul of Grief — 17
5. Choices — 27
6. Something Is Out There — 33
7. High Tides — 39
8. The Siren's Mark — 47
9. Academy for Heroes — 55
10. Hourglass — 69
11. Reckoning — 75
12. Finding Shelter — 83
13. Scars Left — 87
14. Edge City — 91
15. The Lost Prison — 99
16. Nowhere to Hide — 113
17. Chronic: The All-Being — 123
18. Leveling the Playing Field — 127
19. Searching for the Truth — 137
20. Fallen — 141

CHAPTER 1

TJ AND ASHLEY

"Finally." Kratos stepped out of a portal and stared over the edge of Ridge City.

He clenched his fists, and with his eyes closed, he breathed in and opened his eyes after smelling the stench of industry and construction in the city. He couldn't help but smirk and grin at it. He then vanished and quickly appeared in front of an old cemetery, slowly creeping upon an old gravestone with the name "TJ" across it. He gave a snickering smile as he placed his palm and started sliding his fingertips along the top.

"After all these years, not even the great Siren himself could survive," he chuckled.

"You shouldn't be here, Kratos."

Kratos turned around and stood, Ty, wearing an old leather cloak, gave him a snarling glare.

"That is very true. And yet, somehow, I am alive and well."

Ty laughed under his breath and quickly grabbed him by the neck, slamming him against a tall tree stump. Kratos laughed, struggling to escape the tight grip that Ty had around his neck. Kratos took a gulp and only choked.

"We can change that, can't we?" Ty growled.

"There is only one problem with that, Pierman."

Kratos then grabbed Ty's arm, and all he could feel was the scorching pain filling his veins as he dropped Kratos, releasing his grip. Kratos laughed and slowly stood up with a sword in hand. He then pointed it against Ty's throat. Ty must have felt the fear.

"I am not sure how I managed to get resurrected. I do intend to find out," said Kratos.

TY sighed, and Kratos vanished, leaving a patch of smoke behind. TY slowly stood up and stood over TJ's gravestone with a sigh of relief.

"I truly hope that you are still alive, brother."

He then slammed the sword's tip into the ground before the tombstone, allowing it to stay there. Not a move would be made, and there would be no one or anything to knock it over.

Ty then rushed away from the cemetery and was never seen again.

He would hope, anyway.

CHAPTER 2

WHERE EVERYTHING BREAKS

Jace fell to his knees after slamming his fists into a patch of trees. He started to dig his fingernails into the ground, filled with anger deep within. Maybe for most sixteen-year-olds, it would be a normal coming-of-age anger—the "I hate this" kind of anger and "nothing ever seems to go right" scenario.

Yes, much better wording.

Jace was an only child with barely a history. He only knew of his dad being a hero years ago and leaving him and his mother behind.

No explanation.

His parents were true heroes who left that past behind for a better one. Jace stood by his mom every day before she became sick. He hated seeing her in pain. How could he? He had always seen his mom as strong and invulnerable, as if nothing could touch her.

He then heard footsteps approaching his Aunt April, who had watched Jace as a baby when his parents were away.

"It's almost time," she said suddenly.

Jace slowly stood back up and turned facing April. She watched a drip of blood fall to the ground leaving puddles of it. April built tears in her eyes but wiped them away and Jace walked next to her following her to her white SUV heading to Bright Burn Cemetery.

Jace sat quietly in the passenger seat while April kept her eye on him every mile they continued to make. He had nothing really to say without choking up and completely breaking down in tears mentally.

April stopped the car and placed it in the park. Jace felt his body jerk forward and then back before taking his seatbelt off and exiting the vehicle. April sighed and stepped out of the car, following him to the preacher and the group of friends surrounding the casket of Ashley Pierman. Jace felt the nervousness deep down.

It was that feeling where your stomach was turning, but not so much a nauseous feeling. His stomach felt like it was starting to burst, and his heart was slowly breaking—shattering, even.

He and April then sat down in front of the casket, watching as it was lowered six feet under. Everyone tossed roses into the dug-up hole during the preacher's speech, sending her soul away to the heavens, where he knew his mother would probably end up, but he could never be so sure.

The preacher said his final words. Afterward, he closed his Holy Bible and left the cemetery, but not before he placed his hand on Jace's shoulder with a deep sigh and walked away. Jace was the only one left who stayed longer than most.

"Are you sure of this?" Jace heard April speaking to the preacher.

The preacher nodded. "A man needed to see you is what he told me moments before you showed up, ma'am."

April sighed and watched the preacher drive off. April looked up at the grave and saw Jace standing over his mother's grave. She could see that look in his eye: the scared look. The questionable look. She never knew what to truly say to him except that life happens, and he knew his mother would want him to stand strong and hang in there as long as he could.

"I didn't get the chance to say goodbye," Jace thought. "I do not know what I'm going to do, Mom."

April then grabbed his shoulder tightly, and he turned his head to see her smiling. He wiped the tears and looked back at the undug grave. April grabbed his other shoulder and gave it a tap before leaving toward the car. Jace followed not far behind her and closed the door, watching the graveyard workers making their way to the grave as they started mulching and grinding the gravesite.

"She is always going to be with you, Jace," April smiled.

Jace nodded as he watched the car drive away from the cemetery.

CHAPTER 3

A NEW DAY

"Brightburn High School."

The school where every high school kid would decide their lifestyle. Too bad Jace never knew his true calling. All he would ever do was sit in the teacher's classroom with his head on the table while listening to a stranger talk all day and, once in a while, write on the chalkboard.

As the class sat down, Jace noticed that there was no teacher to be seen. He thought maybe they had called in sick and that school was canceled. If only it were that easy.

"Where is the teacher, Jackie?" Jace asked.

Jackie has been a friend of Jace since he started at Bright Burn High. She had been there for him before his mom's passing. Somehow, they clicked as friends.

She shrugged her shoulders. "The principal mentioned something about a new substitute."

Suddenly, they heard the door opening and saw a man who looked a little scrawny. He had that can-do attitude, and his muscles showed more than his shirt sleeves. Jace looked at the man when he turned to face the class. He looked oddly similar to the pictures that he had seen back at home, which his mom had kept for years. He remembered a photo of his parents standing in a group of what seemed to be students, and this man looked almost like them.

"Good morning, class," he said,

Slamming a briefcase onto the desk.

"My name is Tyler Strife, and I will be substituting for you today."

Jace turned to Jackie with his eyebrow lifted, and all Jackie could do was shrug, leaving Jace to turn back around to face the teacher standing over him. He looked the man up and down, wondering how this teacher could be there so quickly.

"You must be Jace Pierman," he assumed.

Jace looked at Mr. Tyler without any fear. He had been taught to be fearless before his mom passed on and because of his history before moving to this school. Jace could feel the steam of his breath slapping him in the face as if it were in close contact, then somehow close enough to touch his cheek.

"Is there much that you would like to share with the class?" he asked.

Jace chuckled, then shook his head.

"I think I'm good."

Mr. Tyler smiled and started marching back to his desk, continuing to talk about a history lesson on Greek gods and how they were something special back in the A.D. era. Jace quietly listened to everything he was saying.

The story of Athena and King Charles, who disagreed on so many things. He wanted to learn so much more. Jackie could see in his eyes that he was intrigued, and she smiled. She hadn't seen him this way since before his mom died. It was as if he were imagining himself in the conversation when Mr. Tyler spoke.

Very intriguing.

The bell then began to ring, and before Jace could exit the classroom, he heard Mr. Tyler talking under his breath. It was as if he were whispering to someone or something. Jace couldn't make out what he was possibly saying. He ignored it and kept walking away with Jackie.

"So, the boy has no idea who he truly is," Mr. Tyler smiled. "All of that is about to change, I'm afraid."

April then approached the guidance office with a bag labeled "Jace's lunch" on the side of it. Jace groaned annoyingly as he grabbed the bag. April smiled and ran her hand through his long brown hair. He rolled his eyes and gave a fake smile.

"Did anything interesting happen today?" April asked.

Before Jace could answer, April turned her attention to Mr. Tyler, who was walking out of the classroom and making his way to the door. April growled quietly and told Jace she would be right back. Jace watched her exit the school, and she shouted,

"Hey!"

Mr. Tyler stopped quickly and slowly turned his head, showing a nervous grin. April crossed her arms and held a nasty, devilish glare.

"So, this is how you expect to get close to him?" April snapped.

"Can we not do this here?" Mr. Tyler sighed.

April scoffed and rolled her eyes.

"Truly, you think I want to even acknowledge you at this very second? The boy cannot possibly be the real reason you are here."

Mr. Tyler turned to April. He could see Jace and Jackie watching them exchange looks back and forth. He did have a reason why he was there, but he could not gather the courage to tell April what was soon going to happen. All he could do was turn his back on her and get into his black SUV.

"Of course!" April exclaimed. "Do what you Piermans do best: run and disappear."

He then started up the car and drove away. Feeling a tear beginning to rush down his cheek, he looked through the rearview mirror as she faded away in a cloud of dust.

April sobbed and turned away, seeing Jace standing at the school window. She wiped the tears away and gave a smile, then got into her car and drove home. Jackie looked at Jace with a curious expression. Jace was not exactly sure what had happened or how April knew the man.

CHAPTER 4

THE SOUL OF GRIEF

Jace stood silently at the kitchen sink. He could hear the sudden laughter echoing from his mother's voice as if he were watching a flashback of when his mother would throw sink water at him while laughing and smiling about it. His mother looked back at him as if she were there, still alive and well. He felt the need to have her there.

April then turned around the corner of the kitchen, seeing him getting lost in his thoughts as she tried calling his name. Jace watched as the flashback vanished, and he turned to April with that look.

"Did you know Mr. Tyler?" he asked.

April sighed, "At one time, I did. How much did you hear?"

Jace scoffed silently. "Enough. How is he a Pierman?"

April stood silent after hearing the one question she didn't think she would ever hear.

"At least not yet."

"There is a lot that you do not know yet, Jace," she told him. "I promised your mom that her past life would not be mentioned."

"Stop pretending that she is still here," he growled. "She is gone, April. I want to know what is going on."

April sighed and stood over an old shoebox. She pulled out a chair, allowing Jace to sit down, and as he did, she opened it up to a photo of Ashley and TJ standing next to a group of what looked like students. She pointed out Ty, who looked exactly like Mr. Tyler.

His mom spoke highly of his dad—all the stories about how he stopped the one evil "Krater" from taking over the Earth to enslave everyone on it. Jace felt that he knew his dad right away, much more than his mom had told him.

He then lifted a folded-up paper in his hand and unfolded it to reveal what was handwritten by TJ. Jace then read:

"Dear Jace, where do I even begin? I know that I left so suddenly, without any given notice. I needed to deal with something so hard to explain, and your mother knew what would happen. I never wanted you to be in that lifestyle as your mother, and I did, but if it ever did come to that, there is something about our family that you need to know. We are what is called a "siren." Three sirens were neither good nor bad, but people only thought of us as nothing but evil. Well, they were not wrong. Every siren has a story and has its endeavor, and the sirens before us caused war, and that exact war seems to be returning. You, my son, may not accept your powers until the time is right. And trust me, if you are anything like your old man, you will know when it is right. Just promise me that no matter how hard you fall, you will never give up. And don't allow the darkness to take over your soul. We may meet again someday, but until then, I love you, son. I know that you will make me proud."

Jace then folded up the letter and chuckled excitedly. He looked up at April as she smiled at him.

Suddenly, the sound of the power lines began to burst outside the house. Jace and April could hear a loud bang echoing down the streets and the lights flickering on and off before the circuit breaker shattered the light bulbs, leaving nothing but darkness all around them.

April looked at Jace and ordered him to hide and stay hidden. She headed downstairs and made her way outside the front door. She saw the street-lights across the street flickering rapidly. She could hear laughter echoing—a burst of familiar laughter. She gave Jace one look, grabbed him in a panic, rushed them both outside the house, and reached the backyard.

"What's happening, April?" he asked panically.

"You need to run, Jace." She warned him. "Do not come back until you know it is safe."

Jace locked onto April's hand. "I am not leaving you. What is going on?"

Suddenly, the house caught fire. Krater slowly stepped through the metal fence, or what was left of it, anyway. He showed that sinister smile and that snarling glare in his eye as he stared down at young Jace.

"So, this is where you have been hiding. Ty seems to be nowhere to be seen," he chuckled.

"You stay away from him," April growled.

Krater laughed and quickly rushed to them, both standing over them like little ants ready to be squashed.

"The last person who ordered me like a dog did not survive to tell the tale." He laughed humbly.

April then pushed Jace away before Krater managed to yank her and pull her up from the ground. Jace never listened, though. He knew how to take a punch, and he refused to let April B be the next family to die. He charged at Krater, only to get caught in his grasp.

"Pathetic."

He threw Jace to the ground and grabbed April's neck tightly, hearing the sound of her neck bones slowly snapping.

"You won't get away with this," April said hesitantly.

Krater gave a grin until the sudden sound of a

fist connecting with his jaw. He dropped April, and Ty quickly grabbed her, laying her on the ground.

"That was not very nice, Pierman," he hissed.

Ty looked at April, seeing the claw marks around her neck. He could hear her slowly losing her breath. Jace quickly crawled over to her, seeing Ty for the first time without a teacher's meat suit around him.

"Stay here," Ty told him.

He then turned around, and all the flames started to swarm around Ty. It was as if he was absorbing the flames to create a burning vortex, and he aimed it toward Krater, knocking him to the ground.

Jace felt April holding his hand tightly. He could feel a blue emerald locked inside a glass vial. She pressed it into his hand, and with the final breath she carried, she pulled him close.

"Do not give up."

She then released his hand, and there was nothing but utter silence.

"April?" he sobbed, trying to wake her up.

Jace then clenched his fist, and with all of that anger coursing through him, his body started to glow a bright blue light, with blue flames rising from his eyelids. Ty and Krater heard Jace yelling angrily and quickly rushed after him. Jace slammed him into the ground, and Ty turned his attention to April's body lying there on the ground.

Jace threw blow after blow and could never force himself to stop. The anger that was held within his siren power took over. He was completely out of control and had no sense of restraint.

Krater then pulled himself away, and he quickly vanished. Jace looked around and noticed that he was finally gone. Ty then looked up to see Jace was gone just like that. Ty placed his head onto April's chest, sobbing, and slammed his fist into the ground.

"Jace, where did you go?"

Ty stood up, looking around, but no sign of him was found.

CHAPTER 5

CHOICES

Jace approached Jackie's two-story window, knocking on the glass, hoping to get Jackie's attention. Jackie looked out and saw scratches on him like he had been in a fight with a group of cats or dogs, if not worse.

"Jace?" She opened the window, allowing him to fall in.

"What happened? You look like some bear attacked you with its claws."

Jace sat there silently. He hid his face in his lap, and Jackie could hear the sudden crying. She sighed and sat next to him, keeping him calm before he looked up.

"April is dead," Jace sobbed. "I don't know what happened, but I felt a power take control, and I wasn't myself. I possibly blacked out, maybe."

Jackie told him to calm down as she laid a metal cot folded out on the floor near her bed. She helped him get on it, then handed him a light bedsheet so he could cover up and rest until morning. Jackie headed downstairs to grab him a glass of water, and as she returned, Jace was out cold, snoring soundly.

Jackie rolled her eyes and gave a smile as she rolled up onto her bed with the covers over her, trapping her in a cocoon.

The next morning, Jace quickly sat up, catching his breath. He saw Jackie brushing her long red hair as she looked at him in her bedroom mirror.

"Thankfully, you are still alive," she said, smiling. "My parents want us at school soon."

Jace took the glass of water and swallowed it down as if he were dying of thirst. He sighed in relief, putting the empty glass down on the floor. He could still feel the tears forming in his eyes, knowing that April was gone along with his mother. He laid his back against the side of Jackie's bed with his head cocked back. The wooden board felt cold along the back of his neck, but he barely noticed.

"You know you didn't have to let me stay here," Jace sighed.

Jackie slammed her hairbrush on the desk, and she stood up, walking over to punch his arm with a growl. Jace shouted in pain, knowing how hard of a right hook Jackie carried.

"Shut up, dummy," she said to him. "You are my best friend, and I am always going to help you out."

Jace chuckled as he rubbed his arm. He then followed Jackie down the stairs and outside. He glanced around, making sure he was not followed from last night. Whoever that man was, he couldn't risk that outburst happening again. He was already afraid, even without notice. He just wanted to get to school and hoped to figure something out.

As they both entered the school's entrance, Jace saw Ty standing there at the trophy case, arms crossed and grief in his eyes. He then looked over to see Jace and Jackie walking toward him. Jace stood there quietly while he waited for Ty to explain who that man was and why he wanted him.

Ty smiled. "You look so much like your dad."

"Did you bury her?" Jace asked. Ty nodded.

"There is so much that you need to know, Jace. You only know half of it."

The school bell then sounded loudly, and all of the students scattered quickly to their classrooms. Jackie sighed and, with a groan, headed to her first class, which she would call her "boring and irritating" science class. Jace started to walk away from Ty before hearing him call his name.

"I don't want to know anything," Jace told him.

Ty sighed and allowed Jace to enter the classroom. Ty knew how hard this was for him. Jace's life was about to change, and it was only just beginning.

CHAPTER 6
SOMETHING IS OUT THERE

After the last bell sounded, Jace stood outside the school. He didn't want to head home or what was left of it. What if that man returned? Would he kill Jace next or spare him long enough to see what this child was made of?

"Jace."

Jace saw Jackie step beside him.

"So, what is your plan now?"

Jace didn't answer. He just stood there quietly with one thing on his mind: the question,

"What is next for him?"

Jace didn't know what to say or how to truly answer that question. Not yet. Jackie smiled, and she saw Mr. Tyler standing behind Jace, giving a slight nod that Jace could only guess meant he was there, glancing.

Jace then turned around to the tall man who was portraying a teacher who had ceased to exist, standing there. He turned his head away with a slight smile.

"What is going to happen now?" Jace asked.

Ty smiled and stared outside the school windows, contemplating what was running through his mind. He could see something inside Jace, and it could have either been a flashback of his dad at that age or the siren that Ty had seen once before. Then again, all Ty could ever see was a spitting image of TJ inside this kid who barely knew him.

"That is truly up to you," Ty told him. "April did not want this new life for you, kid. Your mother didn't want it for you either, but this may be your only chance to find out who you could be."

Jace smiled and turned around. Jackie stood there next to him, giving a smile before she walked away. Ty then held out his hand and Jace started aiming his hand at Ty's until suddenly the lights began to flicker, and the set of doors that led from the school cafeteria slowly opened, revealing a man with his arms hidden behind his back. Steel-toed dress shoes made that clapping sound as they hit the floor.

Ty groaned annoyingly, "Professor Drago."

Drago smirked and eyed the boy and Ty. Drago could see that there was something familiar about Jace, but ignoring that was the best thing for him. Ty could feel the tension in the hall, given the past they had.

"I heard what has happened to your aunt," said Drago. "It must be hard on you."

Ty groaned as he rubbed his eyes.

"What are you doing here, Professor?"

Drago smiled as Jace left them both standing there, discussing whatever that possibly was. He stood next to Ty, taking a glance down the hall, watching as Jace and Jackie faded into the distance with their curious looks.

"Something tells me that Krater has returned," Drago sighed. "Has the kid shown his true power?"

Ty nodded. "Nothing to worry about, though. He is not truly ready to understand what is about to change. We can't force him."

Drago rolled his eyes and started walking away before Ty stopped him.

"Drago, I am serious. You have already done enough while TJ and Ashley were still here."

Drago turned his head. "Oh, and what a joy that certainly was," he said sarcastically.

He then turned away, leaving the school. His

shoes clapped in an echo through the hallways as they started receding away from him. Ty, staring down the hallway, knew Drago was up to something. He was already guessing, but he needed to worry about what would be next for Jace.

Jace and Jackie then strolled down Black Street, only one street away from Jackie's house. Jackie could see the questionable glare in Jace's eyes. So many thoughts ran through his mind, with no answers that he could think of to say.

"What exactly happened last night?" Jackie asked.

"I wish I knew," Jace answered roughly.

Jackie looked further down the road, and for a moment, she swore up and down that she could see a woman just standing there. The woman was wearing a short leather hood, as if she were portraying a knockoff version of "Robin Hood," only with a sword on her back and two daggers attached to her hips.

She tried to show Jace, but when he looked up,

the woman was gone. Jace thought maybe she was getting tired and needed to go home and take a slight nap. Jackie groaned, rubbed her blue eyes, shook them off, and followed Jace back to Jackie's house.

The woman then stood there, watching them recede in the distance, with her hood hiding her long red hair. The only part you could see was the red streaks at the ends of her hair.

"This is the boy we have to keep an eye on?" she thought.

"Yes."

A man with a suit of armor that reflected in the sun looked heavy enough to keep his body down.

"Father knew that this would come. He was not too sure how quickly it would come, though."

CHAPTER 7

HIGH TIDES

Jace told Jackie that he needed to see his family's grave. Maybe seeing them could make him feel somewhat better and give him a better understanding of what this would mean for his future. What is next for him and who he truly will become?

Jackie then allowed him to walk, and she headed back home.

Jace followed the blacktop road through the east of the city and the cemetery that was off the edge of Bright Burn City limits. He stood at the tombstone with his mother's name engraved in bold letters and the day she was born to the day of her death. Then with his father's grave next to it.

The only thing was his was an empty grave and an empty casket. They never found his body, so the only assumption was that he was lost at sea like the last ship of the Bermuda Triangle. Nobody knew where he was or if he was still alive.

Jace then heard footsteps behind him. He turned to see Ty standing next to him with his arms folded behind his back, giving a slight smile. They both then looked over to April's gravestone, which was not far from Ashley's grave. Jace stood quietly before asking what could be next for him.

Ty looked at him with a smile. "Soon enough, all is about to change. I cannot exactly tell you what the future holds for you, Jace."

"So, I just have to let it all flow?" Jace scoffed.

"Your siren heritage is different from your father's and mine," he assured him. "That power will only come when you need it most."

Ty explained to Jace how the sirens were chained together but followed their paths. There was a name for that specific siren, and it could only be carried inside the lastborn—an uncommon and rare name.

Suddenly, they both heard a loud bang at the end of the cemetery entrance. Krater, with a grin on his face, marched up to them. Flames filled the stone heads as he made his way through. Two creatures called "shadow walkers" stood by him, showing their sharp, crooked teeth, and their red eyes brightened the night when the sun made its last scene.

"Jace, stay behind me," Ty ordered.

Krater chuckled, and the shadow walkers surrounded them both, blocking the only exits that could be their escape. Ty tried to find an opening, but none was available.

"It was always going to be this way. You know that." Krater smiled.

Ty held Jace to his back, keeping him calm. But for how long? He could hear Jace's fist clenching and his knuckles making that cracking sound when he was preparing to brawl. The blue aura started to glow brightly, and the flames began heating up in his eyes. Ty had to force the power back and keep it from taking control of him, which was much harder after knowing TJ's blood ran through his veins.

"You have already taken one life, Krater," Ty growled. "Jace is going with me, and you are going to stay far away from him."

Krater clicked his tongue. "That is truly what you think. There are so many hidden secrets under your nose that you can't seem to figure out. TJ was the first, and now where is he?"

Ty quickly rushed after Krater, grabbing him by the neck with his nails digging into him. Falling to the ground, Krater felt his body scraping against the pavement as they reached the streets. Citizens scattered after watching them both toss each other around like a bunch of ragdolls.

Krater laughed and stood up after the last throw that Ty laid on him. "Same old Ty Pierman. High temper when it comes to that family of yours."

"Whose dirty work are you making up for this time?" Ty scoffed.

Krater didn't answer.

He gave a grin and leaped at Ty, grabbing him by the throat and slamming him deep into the ground, bashing his head constantly, hoping he would slowly lose consciousness until he was no longer breathing. Too bad he knew Ty better than that.

Ty then quickly pushed him off, launching him five feet away, and Ty's body was bursting into flames. Krater knew of his siren power after seeing the laughing smile from his teeth. He didn't expect it to be unbelievably exhilarating. He yelled and shouted at Ty, begging him to show that siren family just so it could show him that he was no different from anybody else.

Even Krater himself.

Ty started to march toward him. The ground caught fire, and vehicles around them both exploded into flames with every step he took on the road. Ty tried to attack, but the man and a woman appeared in between them. Krater gave a confused stare before storming off into the distance.

Ty felt the flames die out and his body left scars from the burning fires. Bruising him only for a short time.

"Scarlett and Kade."

They both flipped their hoods back, chuckling.

"If we didn't arrive in time, this could have been your end," Kade smiled.

Ty rolled his eyes and said nothing. Scarlett scoffed and looked to see Jace staring over the far hill from the road. She smiled at him and then looked at Ty with a curious stare.

"That is the wonderful temper that you never learned to control," Scarlett said smartly.

"I was controlling it," Ty ground his teeth.

Scarlett shook her head.

"That is funny."

She then stepped aside, bumping his shoulder as she made her way to Jace, who was frozen there.

At least, that was how he felt.

"Any word on why Krater is even here?" Ty asked.

Kade sighed, "We are still uncertain about it. King Leo saw this coming before his demise, but not this soon."

Kade looked over behind Ty at Jace. "What do we know about the boy?"

Ty turned to Jace and couldn't get the words out from under his chest. He could feel the anger locked in tightly. He just continued to glance at Jace and Scarlett, who was standing with him as she walked him over to Kade and Ty.

Kade knew what he was thinking.

CHAPTER 8

THE SIREN'S MARK

Jace sat at the table inside an old-school diner called "The Tavern."

I suppose it isn't very special, especially the name. It was just a place where Jace and his mom would go for the best hamburgers that they sold there. Scarlett then sat at the table, sliding next to him with a glimmering smile.

Jace sat there quietly.

"Hi, Jace."

The waitress stood at the end of the table with a little notepad.

"What will it be today?"

Jace looked up at her with his finger lifted.

"Just the normal, Andrea."

"Double cheese with crazy sauce. Got it!"

Andrea then headed into the kitchen while Scarlett scoffed under her breath.

"What is so special about the crazy sauce?" she asked.

Jace didn't answer. He only showed a grin and watched as Ty walked through the entrance. Ty stood over Jace, and before he could get a word out, Jace turned away.

"Kade needs me to tend to some issues," Ty sighed.

Scarlett looked at Jace, then back to Ty with that curious look, her hand waving up.

"Say no more," she told him. "I will look after him."

Jace rolled his eyes as Ty left the diner. His eyes then grew wide when he saw Andrea bringing a plate holding a burger with melted cheese in between the two juicy patties under a sesame bun. The crazy sauce covered the beef patties, and you could not tell that there were two patties there. The sauce was brown, like gravy, with a little pinch of pepper seasoning.

Not sure how crazy it could be.

Scarlett couldn't believe her eyes when she saw how it looked. She was surprised at how small Jace was after he devoured it. She almost thought he was going to throw up.

"I hope you know I don't need a babysitter,"

Jace told her after feeling the food hit the bottom of his stomach.

"Is that what you think I am doing?" Scarlett chuckled.

"Jace, you are something special. Being a siren is something great."

Jace laughed, "I am not that special. A siren? C'mon."

Scarlett smiled. "You know, you are probably right. But one day, that power will be your greatest strength."

Suddenly, the doors to the entrance of the diner blasted open, and a group of bikers stormed in. One man was bigger than most of them only because of his giant gut.

Jace groaned. "These guys again?"

Scarlett watched as the men started slapping the women's butts and trying to place their hands around areas that were not needed. The women tried to get away or make them leave, but what was that? Scarlett could tell that.

She then stood up from her seat. Jace tried grabbing for her arm, but she was already in the big man's face with the biggest straight stare on her face. The man stood there with a grin as he watched this new girl staring him down like he was a big target.

"I think you men need to leave," she ordered.

The men laughed as the big man's gut jiggled up and down. You could barely see his lungs when he laughed because his stomach covered most of them.

"Do you know who you are speaking to, little missy?"

Scarlett chuckled, and without a word, the man felt her fist connect with his chin, knocking him to the ground. Jace's eyes grew wide as he saw how hard of a hit the man took.

The bird tattoo along her arm was shining brightly, and her hair burst into bright orange and blue flames. She stood over the man, and the other bikers scattered, then quickly ran from the diner on their motorcycles, driving away like a bat out of hell.

The big man quickly made it to the door and turned his head, pointing his finger.

"This isn't the last you'll hear from me."

He then stormed outside, and everybody in the diner cheered. Scarlett hoped nobody would be afraid and think she was a "freak."

Anywhere else she wound up surely thought so.

Scarlett then sat back down with Jace, and he never took his eye off the bird tattoo along her forearm. It was as if he was drawn to it somehow.

"See?" she smiled. "It comes in handy sometimes."

Jace chuckled and handed the plate to Andrea. He never knew that she was a part of the Siren family.

"Strange," he thought.

They then heard thunder outside. She could feel a rainstorm approaching and quickly left the diner, with Jace following behind her. Where they were going was going to change Jace's life forever.

CHAPTER 9

ACADEMY FOR HEROES

S carlett told Jace to keep his eyes closed until they reached the bottom stair step. He then opened his eyes and he saw a tall building made of glass. The stairs were solid gold. Ancient. He wondered where they were and what this place was.

Academy Zero.

Scarlett would explain about the school being built long before he was born. His parents were the first two to ever attend the school. They fought for the school and ever since then, it has been standing to this day before his very eyes.

Scarlett had him follow her through the school halls, showing every photo of Ashley and TJ holding swords in their hands. Smiles were on their faces, knowing they were just as happy as when Jace was born. He didn't know his dad then, but now he could see his dad somehow. He felt that he was learning about him better.

He knew his mom was somehow right about him.

"Your parents were something special."

Ty startled Jace, and he jumped out of his skin.

"Do you always sneak up on students like that?" Jace gasped.

Ty chuckled, "I cannot tell you how many times your aunt has said that to me."

Jace smiled and looked up at him as he asked about April. How could he have known her?

Ty smiled and explained that they were something

of an item. The academy didn't approve of it, however. April and Ty had to play it off like they never knew one another, which made it hard for Ashley to convince her sister to go for it and make it official already.

"April was an amazing woman," Ty smiled. "But after your parents left here without notice, the council held them accountable for leaving. I was one of those who pushed TJ, my brother, away from here. Well, April disagreed, and since then, we have never spoken again."

"Until that Krater guy came around," Jace scoffed.

Scarlett side-eyed Ty after hearing that. Ty gave a regretful look and continued to brush it off his shoulders.

"I was warned by your father, as was the council. I just never listened." He sighed deeply.

Ty then looked around as if he were searching for something. Or someone. Jace overheard him ask Scarlett where some kid named Brad ran off. Jace saw her shrug her shoulders and roll her eyes annoyingly.

"Something tells me he is getting into some type of trouble," she giggled.

Ty groaned, "Stay with Scarlett, Jace."

He then looked over to see a kid who was maybe slightly scrawnier than Jace but with more meat on his bones, quickly turning around the second he saw Ty's mean, nasty stare in his eyes.

Before Brad could get down the hall, Jace heard Ty raise his voice, and the echo ricocheted off the walls.

"Brad! Here, now."

Brad then stopped and slowly turned around with a sigh, knowing he was busted. He looked into Ty's eyes and smiled nervously.

"I didn't know you were back, Ty," he chuckled.

Ty folded his arms and tapped his foot.

"That is Professor Pierman to you. I know what you were doing. Hand it over."

He then reached his hand out.

Brad groaned and reached into his pocket, handing him a black stone, and Ty grabbed it to place it in his coat pocket. Ty then turned to look at Jace and back at Brad, giving a little smirk and chuckle under his breath. Brad didn't like the way he was staring.

He knew it was about to be either a punishment or a slight relief of pain.

He then walked Brad over to Jace and Scarlett. Seeing Scarlett's sparkling smile on her face, Brad could see the humor in her eyes, even when she knew he had no business stealing some black rock.

"You are going to be young Jace here, a chaperone." Ty chuckled.

Brad's eyes grew wide. "So, I am supposed to become some babysitter?"

"Don't think of it as babysitting, Bradford," Ty laughed. "Think of it as less of a punishment. He is new around here, so don't get him in trouble."

"I hate when you call me that," Brad groaned.

Ty then tapped his shoulder and stepped away with Scarlett following behind him. Brad then scoffed and eyed Jace.

"Well, kid," he told him, "I hope you will get as much enjoyment out of this as I did on my first day."

Jace raised a brow. "Kid? Who does he think he is speaking to like that?"

Jace clearly could tell that Brad was maybe a year or two younger than he was. But he just brushed it off and followed Brad down the hall, seeing the classrooms that held students either sitting down listening to lectures or where students would fight each other one-on-one. He could hear Brad going on about how the fighting class could help release the anger that others carry for the rest of their lives.

Jace then stopped in the middle of the hallway, staring at a statue that seemed to be a man holding a woman's hand in the sky. Or at least, that was what it looked like. The statue showed the man and woman reaching for each other, but they were close and seemed so far away.

Brad noticed him looking and gave a smile.

"Alec and Sylvia were the sirens that led this place long ago."

Jace smiled. "What happened to them?"

Brad scoffed excitedly and began the history lesson about how Alec was an orphan. Nobody knew of his parents or where he possibly came from. Later on, Alec was taken in by King Leo, ruler of the Elder Isles, and at that time, they found out that Alec was known as the Elder Siren. He went on to add that Alec was the first siren centuries after what was called the "Great War," started by the ancient siren.

"Alec then discovered an unknown woman named Sylvia Scarlett. She was not exactly a siren, per se. Before Alec knew what she would truly become, they were in love. The council of gods didn't agree, but they brushed it off. Alec and Sylvia eventually had two boys, and after the birth, everything changed."

Jace continued to listen. Brad continued by describing how Sylvia started a war against Alec and the Isles. Alec tried to stop her and convince her that she could end it all if she would just come up with a reason.

Brad tried to finish the story until Ty cleared his throat. Jace and Brad turned and saw Professor Drago standing next to him, grinning after hearing the story.

"There is more to that story," Ty chuckled.

Brad smiled and walked away, leaving Jace with Ty and Drago.

Drago looked Jace up and down with a grinning smile.

"You are going to like it here, kid."

Drago then left the two alone, staring at the statues. Ty hid his hands behind his back, giving a smile and seeing Alec's golden face glancing up at Sylvia. It was as if he could see them trying so hard to hold each other's hands. He could feel it.

"You said that there was more to the story," Jace reminded him. "Who exactly was he?"

Ty felt his breath shudder, and his voice started to crack.

"He was our father. Your grandfather. Brad was right about the story and Sylvia did certainly change after the birth of your father and me. Your grandfather didn't notice it until it was too late. There was darkness evolving inside her, and some noticed. King Leo noticed, as did the ones who worshipped him. Now, TJ and I were only kids before Sylvia returned after being banished, no thanks to a man named Jonah Blackheart. He was only a human at the time, and he was the only one who believed Sylvia had done the right thing."

"He was someone who lived on the island?" Jace interrupted.

"Yes," Ty continued, "he was the one who brought Sylvia around, and she waged what was called the 'dark war.' Blackheart was a part of it all, and Sylvia was so powerful with him by her side that Alec could only do so much. But like any other messiah, the gods watched over him, and they were his source of power. They trapped our mother, and after that, we never saw her again. We only knew her for a short time because Alec thought it was the right thing to do for their kids."

"What does any of this have to do with me?" Jace asked.

Before Ty could answer, he heard the doors open. Groaning, Jace could see the annoying look in his eye. A man, who had the tone of somebody who was British and was wearing a white lab coat, stood at the doors, clanking at the scenery with a bright smile as if he was welcomed.

Ty then grabbed the man by the chest and

pushed him against the wall. The man chuckled excitedly after feeling the force of his back slamming against the concrete wall.

"It is always great to see you, Ty," he chuckled.

Ty tightened his grip, pushing all of his strength against him.

"Give me one reason why I should not kill you where you stand."

The man laughed, "Well, I am lifted from the ground."

Ty growled and stepped away angrily.

"Strike, this is serious."

Strike scoffed, "Look, I know what I have done in the past is unforgivable."

Ty stopped and turned with a silent stare.

He was trying his best not to grab Strike and choke him until he turned black and blue, then croaked. It would only make matters worse. He looked down the hall, seeing that Jace was and watching everything. Ty sighed.

"Unforgivable?" he whispered. "You turned on TJ and Ashley. It was your fault that Krater was able to come into this school and practically destroy it—everything my father built in this school."

"And now Krater is somehow back from his slight banishment," Strike scoffed.

Ty's eyes grew wide.

"This is worse than we thought, Ty," he told him. "It is strange how you have not figured it all out yet. How could Krater possibly be alive?"

"Not this again," Ty muttered. "If Drago had anything to do with that, don't you think I would have figured it out a long time ago?"

Strike scoffed under his breath, "You truly believe that?"

He then glanced at Jace, who was still staring at them both, unable to take his attention away from two grown men looking as if they were about to kill each other.

"Drago is the key to everything, Ty. I think you already know, and TJ was right for once in his life. But Krater destroyed everything before you could even blink."

Ty stood silently. He then pointed to Jace, asking him to come down the hall. Jace stood firmly. Silently.

"Jace, this is Professor Strike," Ty sighed. "He is going to be looking after you for a while."

Strike's eyes grew wide, and he stuttered as if he hadn't asked to volunteer. Ty chuckled, giving the craziest grin after choosing him. It felt like a punishment for what he had done in the past, but Ty was never that type of person. He was never the torturing type.

"If you want to let bygones be bygones, this is your chance," Ty told him.

Strike glared.

"You are enjoying this, aren't you?"

Ty walked away silently, still wearing the grin on his face.

Strike gave a soft chuckle and waved his arm as Jace followed behind him.

CHAPTER 10

HOURGLASS

Jace followed Strike into a large room that looked like a lab. Jars held strange insects in dirty water. Some moved around and were still alive, while others were just there—dead. Jace tapped his finger on one of the jars to watch the little creature wiggle, but no sign of disgust came to mind for Jace.

"So, you finally learned who you are," Strike smiled.

Jace nodded and sat down on a long pull-out bed. Strike planted himself in a rolling chair and rolled around the room, searching for folders lined up along the bookshelves.

You would think it would carry books, but strangely enough, it had more folders than the Mississippi River.

Strike then rolled back over to Jace with a needle in hand and grabbed his arm. He wrapped some stretchy tape around his arm and tightened it until the vein in his left arm began to pop out, becoming visible. Then he slowly stuck the needle into his arm hearing the painful sound rushing through Jace's breath.

Jace tried not to look at the blood being drawn from his arm into the skinny tube, filling it to the top, almost overfilling it. Jace couldn't help but ask what he was drawing blood for.

Strike smiled and quickly plucked the needle out. Jace shouted in pain, and Strike covered the blood oozing from the small hole that he had poked through with a white bandage, wrapping it around the wound.

"I have done this many times with your mother. She always knew how to get hurt, and the wraps that she wore were outnumbered." He chuckled.

Jace smiled. "She was always stubborn. She could take a hit."

Strike nodded as he finished the bandage and laid the roll on Jace's bedside.

"Your father was her only obsession. She loved that man, and when she was injured, she never wanted to tell him. He would kick the ass of whoever laid a hand on her." He laughed.

Brad then knocked on the door.

"Ty wanted to make sure that you had that blood sample ready."

"Ty or Drago?" he muttered.

Brad rolled his eyes. "He knew you would ask that, and he would give his reply: 'Shut up and get it to him.'"

Strike then scoffed at Brad and tossed the vial to him. Luckily, Brad could catch rather well.

He then left the lab, and Jace looked up at the top bookshelf at a tall hourglass. It looked like it was made centuries ago. The dust and dirt were written all over it, and it and it had never lost time. The sand was still full at the top, but only half of it was filled at the bottom. It made no sense, at least not to Jace, anyway.

Strike then noticed his attention to the hourglass and gave a smile.

"That was a gift from your grandmother before she went completely dark on us. She said that it was a sign of the end of time. When it stopped and was only halfway full, it meant the end. Since then, the hourglass has stopped exactly at that."

Strike then heard Drago's voice come over the intercom, calling for him to rush to him immediately. Strike groaned as he knew what he most likely meant and what he needed most.

After Strike left Jace alone in the lab, Jace roamed around the school hallways, peeking inside each doorway he could find, only to discover many rooms. He finally opened one door that had a demonic tail symbol on it, and he saw a little boy just sitting there.

The boy quickly looked up with a startling gasp.

"Who are you?"

"I'm Jace," he smiled. "I'm sorry. I didn't know that anyone was staying here."

The boy smiled and continued to read a book that he held in his hand. Jace couldn't help but wonder what made the book so interesting. The boy watched him glance around the room.

"Do you have a name?" he asked.

The boy smiled and looked up.

"Ryan."

Jace smiled back, and he looked at the shelves of old mythology books and books based on the Greek wars and everything there was to know.

"You seem to have a lot of history in your life," Jace smiled.

Ryan nodded. "Ty gave them to me. He said that he no longer needed them so he knew I could get some use out of them."

Jace then heard Ty knock on the door, giving a smile.

"Ryan, is everything all right?"

Ryan nodded and smiled. Ty gave a nod, and Jace followed him out of the room.

CHAPTER 11

RECKONING

Strike then entered the room. Drago stood in front of a pedestal, holding the vial that carried Jace's blood in the air. He heard Strike's footsteps approaching and gave a slight smirk after turning his head.

"You did well delivering this to me," he smiled.

Strike scoffed and closed the door behind him.

"You told me before I was banished that there was nothing to worry about. I saw that evil glare in your eye, Drago."

Drago rolled his eyes and laid the vial down. He

turned to Strike after seeing the door was sealed shut. He had a feeling Strike was beginning to trust him less than he had before.

"Did you finally figure it out?" he chuckled. "Yet, no living soul believes you."

Strike felt his breath beginning to tremble. Nervous, even. He was finally confronting Drago and fearing for his life after looking at the man.

"How long did you know?" Drago asked.

Strike took a gulp. He felt his Adam's apple lift from the bottom of his neck up near his chin before speaking.

"It took me a while to put the pieces together," he scoffed. "TJ warned me after warning Ty. I thought to myself, why would our headmaster of the school that Alec had sworn to leave under protection want to cause something that was crazy? Then, days after the attack at Ashley's home, where Jace was able to stop Krater and allow him to escape, Krater visited me. "I didn't believe it until I saw Jace that night of April's death, and when Krater showed up, it was no coincidence." He told me about Blackheart and the plan. "You were the true heir to pull it off."

Drago smiled. "Well, at least someone was able to figure it out. Not much longer, and Krater will be blasting through those windows. This school will be rubble, and no survivors."

Strike's eyes grew wide. "How long?"

Drago chuckled, and without notice, the lights flickered off and then back on, leaving Strike all alone. Strike growled, and then the sudden loud "BOOM" echoed outside the school.

Running through the halls, gathering the students, and shouting for everyone to move and evacuate the school immediately, Ty and Jace stood at the steps of the entrance, watching drones flying through the sky and the windows shattering all over the floor.

Ty held Jace, Brad, and the students back behind him as the glass fell to the floor.

"Strike, what is happening?" Ty shouted.

"Drago. Krater." He panicked.

Suddenly, a knife swiped Ty's shoulder blade. He then fell back, and Krater charged in. A man stood near him, wearing some type of tech from head to toe. A red eye was engraved into his chest.

"This is the kid. The so-called siren?" the man scoffed. "Ivan, search the place. Drago wants to make sure that it comes down to killing anybody. No survivors."

The eye around the man's chest then ejected from it and formed into a drone. It groaned and flew around the schoolyards.

"Who are you? A lackey doing Krater's dirty work?" Ty asked.

The man laughed hysterically. "My name is Quick Shot. My real name is irrelevant. Not that it will matter to you."

Quick Shot and Krater then exchanged looks,

and Krater pushed Ty back, then grabbed Jace by the throat, lifting him from the ground with a smirk.

"I knew there was something special about you, kid," Krater laughed. "I truly wonder what makes that little power tick."

Jace groaned and struggled, trying to get out of this man who was just holding him up tightly. Jace could feel the power coursing through his body, but somehow it just would not come out.

Ty then quickly charged, grabbing Krater by the waist, and Jace dropped to the floor with Brad pulling his arm to get them away. Quick Shot gave a groan, and with the press of a button on his arm, shadow walkers jumped and growled. He then gave the command for them to enjoy the feast in other words.

Krater then felt his body scrape across the floor. He stood up, wiping blood from his bottom lip with a grin and a laugh.

"You will not survive this," he cackled.

Ty then grabbed him by the neck, lifting him off the ground.

"Can't you see, Ty? Drago wants to be sure that you are gone so your little nephew can live without anybody. You cannot protect him any longer."

Ty then turned and saw Drago standing there with a .45 mm pistol in his hand.

"Drago?" Ty scoffed. "A gun?"

Drago smiled and cocked the loaded gun back, placing his finger on the trigger.

"I am not going to expose the power that I possess, Ty. It is just a shame it took you so long to find out. Strike knew before you did; speaking of which, Krater being choked is what he gets for ruining the true plan."

Krater shrugged. Ty then slammed Krater to the ground and raised his hands in the air.

"I didn't want to believe it. Alec mentored you and this is how you repay him?" Ty's voice shook.

Drago chuckled, and before he could pull the trigger, the walls started to crack, and the school was close to crushing everyone. Drago dropped the gun and vanished, as did Krater. Ty looked around with tears falling from his eyes.

He could hear April's voice somewhere out in the open. He looked around but saw nobody—only the voice telling him that it was over and this was Jace's turn now.

The school walls then blew, and cement blasted everywhere, leaving dust in the wind. Ty gave a smile before vanishing into the dust, leaving his body somewhere under all that rubble.

CHAPTER 12

FINDING SHELTER

Jace and Brad ran down the hallways, banging on the classmates' doors and shouting, "Get out of the school!" throughout the building. They heard the school shaking suddenly, feeling as if an earthquake was taking place.

Ryan rubbed his eyes, and Jace grabbed him, running quickly. The shadow walkers' growls were loud enough that they sounded close.

"Where is the nearest place to seek shelter?" asked Jace.

Brad was too busy catching his breath to even

answer. Ryan knew of the tunnels under the school and led them there as quickly as he could. Once every single student was in the tunnel and close together, Brad stood over Ryan.

He could hear the fear coming from his voice, and Ryan tried not to shake. He told him not to come out of these tunnels. He was not sure where they might be or if they would return for them.

The quakes then finally ceased, and the shadow walkers were no longer hunting. Brad looked at Jace, but Jace shrugged.

Jace and Brad heard footsteps that sounded like they were running at a fast pace. Strike quickly stopped, seeing the boys were okay along with the classmates. The look on his face though, made Jace and Brad tell it was not a good sign.

Jace and Brad then followed him to the entrance of the school. The glass was completely shattered, and what used to be the school walls were broken down. The poles that held the school up were hanging from the power lines and outside the windows. It was like a massacre. It was unbeliev-able that it was a school.

Jace and Brad then followed Strike to a room where Drago's last presence was. When they arrived, their eyes grew wide as they saw Ty's body under the rubble. Brad stood there, retching almost, while Jace couldn't look. He felt tears starting to build up in his eyelids.

"Drago vanished before it happened. Krater too," Strike told them. "I couldn't stop it."

"We need to leave the school soon," Brad admitted. "Knowing that floating drone, or whatever Ivan is, could be back to sweep the area any minute."

Jace then stopped Brad.

"What about Ryan?"

Brad shrugged. "They are safe, and they won't come out until everything is clear."

Jace stayed quiet and left the room. He then

walked down to the tunnel, opening the vault where the students were locked up. Ryan could tell something was going on, but he ignored it. Jace smiled and gave Ryan a small dagger with the initials "AP" engraved on the handle.

"Keep this as long as you can," he told him. "It will keep you safe."

"What about you guys?" he asked.

Jace sighed. "You kids are survivors. This school taught you everything you needed to know about how to fight and protect, yeah?"

The kids nodded. Jace then smiled and opened the door, leaving it wide open. Ryan knew that was a sign that it was clear, and he needed to be cautious.

Especially now.

CHAPTER 13

SCARS LEFT

Drago and Krater stood on the mountaintop, outside a darkened cave. Drago sighed and looked at Krater.

"Are you sure this is where the last piece is located?" he asked.

Krater nodded. "Blackheart's remains are in there."

Drago then whistled, and a shadow walker appeared by his side.

"Greta, you know what to find."

The creature grunted and ran through the cave. After minutes of searching, the creature held a book in its mouth. Drago took the book and opened it to find a black stone that was pure and showed a heart upside down. Black goo filled the vial, and Drago grinned, knowing that this was it.

"Do we have a plan for bringing him back?" Krater asked.

Drago groaned. "Of course. Did you find our young darling yet?"

Krater shook his head. "The last she told me was that she was delivering Scarlett to the prison."

Drago raised a brow. "That prison is still around? Angel hated that place before and after being sent there by Fiona and Leo."

"She stated that we would know if she needed us," Krater added.

"Hm," Drago hummed. "I truly hope she knows what she is doing. In the meantime, we must be ready for the Dark Lord's return."

Krater then followed Drago to Atlas City. They stood in front of an old, abandoned tech lab.

Cybertek.

"Why are we here?" Krater grunted.

"This scientist long ago made a machine that could resurrect anybody he wanted to," Drago explained.

"It worked. He brought back his son from the dead, but he was more robotic than human. I will explain everything later; we need to get it started."

Krater then followed Drago into the building, and the lights from the Cybertek sign flickered. The doors closed behind them and it turned dark.

CHAPTER 14

EDGE CITY

Jace and Brad followed Strike through the woods and city lights. They took the trains that would race through Manhattan and New York City before reaching the last city that was only eighty miles out from the Great Apple.

Edge City.

The city was in the name. It was on the edge of the map and not many people knew about it. It showed on the Welcome to Edge City sign population of 3,000 written on it. Strike had refuge there in case he would ever need tools or just a place to crash and hide.

"Strike, where are we?" Brad asked.

Strike then locked the door quickly, giving a smile.

"My home. Edge City was where I was born and raised before Alec took me in."

Jace sat down quietly. He could feel flashbacks of when his mother was still alive, and it was just him and her training. Learning. Laughing.

He then heard Brad calling out, trying to get his attention. Jace looked up and wiped a tear from his eye.

"So, what do we do now?" he asked.

"If I can find the location of the Isle of the Gods, then maybe Kade can figure something out. I just never thought Drago would be able to attempt what he plans to attempt."

Brad asked him what he meant. How could he explain the events that were prophesied ages ago were coming true? It was a lot to manage.

"The students will rebuild," Brad smiled. "Whatever is coming, it's coming fast."

"This is just too much."

Jace stood up and stormed off, pacing back and forth.

"Ty is dead because of whatever is next for me. There had to be something that we could have done. I am not a hero."

Strike sighed, "True."

Jace groaned and scoffed under his breath.

"Someday, you will be. Finding Kade is your only chance if you are meant to be ready. Krater, then Drago, and after that, it will only get worse."

"There was nothing we could do, Jace," Brad assured him.

Jace shook his head and continued outside in the pouring rain. He made his way into the city streets, which were in the middle of Edge City.

Kicking rocks from under his feet, his long curls were drenched and hung over his face.

He couldn't stop sobbing. He tried to hide it, and it was easy with the rain just dripping.

"Why? I needed you, Dad. What have I ever done to deserve this?" Jace sobbed.

Suddenly, he felt a cold breeze pass by, and he looked around, but nothing was there. He then heard a voice, a woman's voice, echoing vaguely in his mind. He groaned and held his hand against his forehead as he fell to his knees. He saw Scarlett chained up in a cell somewhere.

Blood dripped from her bottom lip. Her wrists had scars all the way around. She looked up, and it was as if she could see him. It was like he was there with her.

"Scarlett?" he muttered.

"Lost Prison," she whispered. "Please, hurry."

He then felt a hand touch his shoulder. He

jumped and flipped a woman to the ground. She gasped as he threw her body down, and he quickly got up, freaking out.

"I am so sorry," he gasped.

The woman chuckled as she slowly stood up.

"Don't worry about it. It's the first time a guy has managed to throw me over his shoulder, though."

The rain then stopped. Clouds broke up and revealed the sun as it blinded Jace's eyes. The woman then grabbed his arm and dragged him to the edge of town just so they could get out of the rain.

"You seemed stressed back there," she told him as she took a swig of red cherry soda. "Do you have a name?"

Jacc chuckled. "Jace. Jace Pierman."

"Jade is the name," she smiled. "So, what was a guy like you doing out there by yourself?"

Jace looked at the city. "I'm not sure," he told her.

Before Jace could say any more, Brad and Strike rushed up to the top side of the hill where they were sitting. Strike scoffed after seeing Jade. Jace wondered who she was. Brad was too busy to notice, as he was trying to tell Jace that the jet was ready and that they were trying to find him in the process.

"Why am I not surprised?" Strike smiled.

Jade rolled her eyes and started to walk away before Strike raised his voice.

Jade stopped and turned around. "Look, I just saw the guy on his knees, feeling like he was getting a headache. I'm not sure why you care; you abandoned me."

Jade rushed off, and Strike stood there watching. Jade was his daughter, believe it or not—a life that was never explained.

"Edge City." His mistaken life.

"We leave now," Strike ordered. "The Isle of the Gods is going to be a long flight."

Jace then grabbed Strike's arm. He explained that he saw Scarlett, and she seemed to be in trouble. He mentioned the "Lost Prison," and when he said it, Strike's eyes grew wide, and he quickly turned away with Brad and Jace following behind him to the jet.

The hatch then closed behind them and shot off through the clouds.

Edge City.

Jonathan Strike looked away. He turned away.

CHAPTER 15

THE LOST PRISON

The jet started to soar through the skies. Jace and Brad saw the clouds opening and blue ocean waters filling the horizon. It created a beautiful scenery as if they were in heaven.

The closer they were getting to the islands; the beaches were large and wide. You couldn't tell from the distance with how small it looked from afar until you came close it was the greatest thing you had ever seen. Strike sighed and smiled.

Jace was relatively excited to see the Isles for the first time. He had never been so far away from home until now. His mother had told him so many stories about this place, and now that he could see it with his own eyes, it was everything the stories had described.

"I hope you are right about Scarlett, Jace," Strike told him. "I just want to know how Kade let it slip."

The jet then landed in front of Ryker's Castle. Kade marched down with his soldiers marching beside him. He wore shiny black armor that could blind a person.

Strike, Jace, and Brad waited for the hatch to lower down. Jace asked Strike who Jade was and what she meant by abandoning her. His being a father was explanatory, but the daughter's story was hard to get past.

Strike ignored it and continued. Strike shook Kade's hand and they followed him into the castle, explaining about Scarlett and her disappearance to the Lost Prison.

Kade sighed. "I knew something was wrong. She hasn't called in for days."

He slammed his hands on the table.

"Right now, we need to get there and rescue her," Strike recommended. "Jace and Brad will get in and find her."

Kade chuckled, "It may be easy to get into the prison. The gods made that prison, so believe me; it is hard to escape it. There is also someone who lurks around the prison that my mother put away long ago."

He then looked at an old photo with Scarlett, himself, King Leo, and Queen Fiona standing inside a courtroom-like setting.

A woman stood across from them, chains holding her wrists together and a lock without the keyhole locked around the cuffs. Kade explained the trial of Angelina, Fiona's sister, for treason. He added that she had attempted to kill almost everybody in the court of Kings and Queens, including her sister and brother.

"Our mother sent her to the Lost Prison for all of eternity. Drago and Krater must have helped her escape, and she took Scarlett there. She is dangerous, and Scarlett is powerless when the dark angel appears."

"What do you mean she is powerless?" asked Jace.

Kade then handed Strike a holographic map and gave a deep sigh, trying to hold back tears from drawing out.

"You will have to wait and see. There is no time to explain."

Before Jace could even get another word out, Kade quickly rushed them off to the jet and stepped away as the jet left the Isles. Strike placed the coordinates into the navigational system, and then a loud slam from Jace's hand landed on the control board.

"Is there a problem, Jace?" Strike scoffed.

"I want to know why Kade isn't trying to save his sister on his own," Jace growled. "This is pointless. We should be going after Krater and ending this."

Strike rolled his eyes. "You are not ready to take him on, and you certainly do not have the power to stop Drago. It is going to take some time, kid. We are killing the time, and this is how we must do it."

Jace groaned. "I never asked for any of this. I lost my mom, my aunt, and now Ty. If I lose another, I am not sure if I can become this so-called hero everyone thinks I am supposed to turn out to be."

Strike smiled and he called for Brad. Brad held a giant book that looked like an old photo album from the 1960s or maybe earlier. He opened it up and stood Ashley with TJ's hand over her shoulder, a smile glowing in black and white.

"They looked so happy," Jace smiled.

Strike smiled. "It certainly was."

Jace then came across a photo that had students standing by a brick wall. Drago was on the far right, while a woman was on the far left of him. She wore a dark leather jacket, and her hair was black with red highlights, which Jace pointed out.

"Her name was Jessica. She never had a last name, but she and your mother were not exactly 'hiking buddies,'" Strike explained.

"Who was she?" Brad asked.

Strike scoffed and quickly turned to the other pages, ignoring the question. He pointed his finger at Drago's smug face as he stood with Alec, shaking his hand. Strike was quiet and stared at the photo for a long time.

He then saw the jet slowly approaching the prison, and he slammed the book shut and placed it down on the table. It landed on top of a field that was far east of the prison and out of plain sight.

Brad and Jace then left the jet and started to cross what was called "The Abyss of Agony." Legend had it that you could hear the cries of souls who died at the bottom—fallen souls who could never be reached or saved.

Brad stood for a moment, hearing the cries. Or at least he thought he was hearing them. He was walking shakily across it, doing his best to ignore them. Jace didn't seem to be bothered by it; he was too focused on finding Scarlett and hoping that it wasn't too late.

"Now remember you two," Strike's voice echoed, "getting in is the easy part. Escaping is the hard part. I may not be able to help you."

Brad and Jace nodded as they approached the prison gates. The gates began to open loudly, giving a loud screech as they scraped against the ground. Brad looked at Jace, and Jace looked on as he headed inside, passing the gates.

They heard the gates closing behind them, startling Brad, who jumped a couple of feet ahead of Jace. Jace couldn't help but grin and let out a slight laugh before covering his mouth and telling Brad to shut up.

"No turning back now," Jace sighed.

Brad tried calling for Strike the farther they powered through the prison of empty cells, and he heard nothing but static. Jace and Brad knew they were on their own.

They then heard a sudden groan echo through the halls. Of course, it was dark, and they could barely see where the mysterious groaning was coming from. Jace stopped and could hear Scarlett's voice in his mind.

They were close.

Suddenly, they heard movement pass by, and a low growling sound echoed nearby.

"Please tell me that was your stomach, Jace," Brad said nervously.

Jace shook his head and quickly turned to a black-coated wolf creeping near them. Sharp teeth glistened under the moonlight. When there was one wolf, they both knew there was a pack. A sudden giggling sound echoed behind the wolves as they backed away just for Angelina to slowly walk between them.

"My, what was a surprise," she giggled. "Alec's little grandson and a lackey. I was told that you would show, but who knew it would be this soon?"

Jace clenched his fist.

"Where is she?" he growled.

Angelina giggled. "No need to be so defensive. This prison is nothing like any ordinary prison. It strips your powers, and that includes your siren heritage."

Jace scoffed and gave a grin.

"I can still punch."

He then charged at Dark Angel, throwing every punch and kick he could.

Angelina was no match for Jace, however. She swung his body from left to right, then forced him back. He could hear Brad shouting for him. Jace was useless without his power, and Angelina knew it. She wanted this moment.

Angelina then cringed as her head turned away. Hearing Scarlett's annoying cry entered her mind.

"Leave them out of this," she begged her. "Please."

Angelina groaned and with a snap of her fingers, she was gone. Brad helped Jace up and they both saw an open cell. Jace pointed,

"She is there."

Whispered from his breath.

He could hear Scarlett moaning and groaning. She was calling out to him. They both then entered the cell, and Scarlett was on her knees, chained up. Scarlett looked up with a slight laugh.

"Get me out of here. She will be back."

Scarlett suddenly felt pain rushing through her heart.

It was as if she was being damaged somehow. Angelina then appeared behind them with a nasty grin.

"This is what Kade must have meant," Brad worried.

"Did you truly think I would allow you to get out that easily, little niece?" she chuckled.

She clicked her tongue. "You better be lucky I allowed them to find you. Getting out is the hard part, and I cannot let that happen."

She then charged at Jace. Brad felt his body being forced against the wall, pushing away from Scarlett and Jace. Jace stood up, brushing blood from his shirt, and Scarlett was still screaming in agonizing pain. She could not get away from the "dark angel." Not this time.

Suddenly, the sound of blades was muffled through the ceiling of the prison before the jet's engine started to destroy it. Strike's voice then came over the intercom, and Jace quickly jumped at Angelina, grabbed her waist, and slammed her to the ground. She strained as Jace held her down.

Brad then grabbed Scarlett, and Strike landed the jet on a debris of rock and cement. Releasing the hatch for Brad to board the jet. He turned around yelling for Jace but Jace was too mad and pushed Angelina to the ground.

Brad quickly rushed down and grabbed him, telling him it was not worth it. They had to hurry and get out of there while they still could.

After that, Strike pulled the jet up, flying away from the prison with Angelina glaring up at them, laughing, and she heard Krater's heavy footsteps approaching behind her.

"This time is going to be your moment," she told him. "If he gets to full strength, Krater, you could be the next to die."

Krater smiled. "Drago wants the boy to reach his full potential, Angel. This is not about me, and as long as Blackheart returns, then Drago will not care. Drago wants the boy for himself, even if that means he has to lose many who are closer to him. Jace will soon suffer, and he will have one option."

"What option?" she raised a brow.

Krater said nothing and smiled. He then left the prison, and not long after, so did Angel.

CHAPTER 16

NOWHERE TO HIDE

As Strike guided the jet back to the Isle of the Gods, Jace handed Scarlett a cold glass of water. She chugged it down like she had been dying of thirst for over a century. She threw the glass down, hearing the glass shattering across the ground.

"I am not sure what would have happened if you hadn't rescued me sooner," she groaned.

"Who knew I would be the one saving you?" Jace chuckled.

Scarlett smiled. "How long until we reach the Isle, Jonathan?"

Strike could see the horizon passing through the clouds, and the island shores filled the area beautifully. Scarlett sighed with relief.

The jet then landed. Kade stood outside, waiting for his sister to come running out and hug him, or at least acknowledge him somehow.

But she only gave him the face of anger. She said nothing and continued into the castle.

"She isn't happy," Strike sighed.

Kade chuckled and started to head into the castle.

Scarlett stood at Queen Fiona's statue, silently. Kade stood next to her with his arms crossed, giving a slight smile.

"After all of these years, I thought Mom was such a hero. Somebody who I could look up to as a person. As royalty," Scarlett scoffed.

"Instead, I found out that she was just like everyone else: Father, too."

"What exactly did Angelina tell you?" Kade asked.

Scarlett glared at him. "Everything. Our mother was not a saint, brother."

Kade sighed and turned away.

"You know that is a lie, Scar."

Scarlett chuckled. "Angelina was able to hurt me. Now, why is that? She overpowered me, and she told me that our mother, of all people, had done many wrongs before, including giving up a child who never knew about us."

"She could have lied," he told her.

"Auntie has always been a liar, but this time, in her voice, she was speaking nothing but the truth." Kade was quiet.

Scarlett shook her head and quickly stormed out of the hall. Kade looked up at Fiona's statue, the eye pointing down, staring directly at him. He knew and couldn't say a word about it.

"Young nephew."

Kade then turned, and Angelina stood there with a grin on her smile. Kade gasped and took a step back.

"How did you get here?" he asked, panicked.

Angelina clicked her tongue. "I believe you already know, youngling. Krater wants to take this time to unleash whatever possible power the young Pierman boy possesses."

Suddenly, the ground began to rumble. The ground outside the castle started to crack in half, and Strike's jet fell between it. Krater and Angelina wanted to be sure nobody would get off of the island.

While Kade was focusing on Angelina, Jace and Brad looked around, hearing the castle walls starting to crumble. Strike yelled after watching his nice black jet vanish into the void as if the world was eating it whole.

Jace then saw Krater standing there inside the

castle with his arms crossed and a grin that only children should be afraid of. Jace looked over at Brad and Strike, hoping they would allow this to be his moment. Strike nodded with no care in the world.

Brad didn't want to allow it. Strike told him that he had to finish "Krater" and then "Drago." There was no other way.

Strike and Brad then took a step back. Krater laughed and lowered his arms to his sides. Jace could feel the power rushing through him, but it wasn't enough.

Not yet.

"This is something, isn't it?" Krater chuckled. "Your father stood exactly as you do, hoping he could take me down with every inch of his power."

Jace stayed silent. His fists then gave a blue flame that formed around them, and Krater's eyes glared down, giving an excitable grin. He could already feel the anger rising.

Jace then took one foot behind the other and launched himself at Krater. Jace grabbed him around the waist, slamming him down to the ground. He threw Krater outside the doors, and Krater landed on the edge of the beachside. He felt sand filling up his palms as he slowly stood up. Krater already had a scar swiped across his left cheek by a kid who had just now started to show his true colors.

Jace then stormed out of the castle and stood across from Krater. Blue flames covered his eyes, and his body was different this time. Somehow, the fire was burning his clothes and creating a power suit that was shaded with black and a mixture of blue plastered all over it.

Krater couldn't believe what he was seeing. It was completely new, and he had never seen a siren able to do that.

"I knew that there was something special about you, Jace," he said nervously.

Jace started walking closer, and Krater could only go so far without diving into the ocean waters.

He then stopped and stood inches close to Krater. Krater gave a smile and clenched his rough, oversized fist, not giving a flinch, and he charged at Jace.

Jace then grabbed him by the neck, stopping him in his tracks. Krater struggled to escape it. The siren's strength was just too much, and Krater knew it.

"Go ahead, siren. Do what your family could not," Krater begged.

Jace then closed his eyes, and Krater felt his soul-crushing. It was as if his soul was being sucked down through a black hole, and arms were wrapping around it until it was complete darkness. Krater looked into Jace's eyes with a chuckle.

"Looks to me like you are ready."

Krater's body then turned to complete ash, and

a ball of light lifted into the air and then turned into black smoke.

The flames then burned out, and Jace chuckled as he felt the suit around his chest. It seemed like he finally had control over his siren power.

He then turned around, and Angelina held a dagger against Strike's pointy throat. She readily slit it and created a bloodbath, wearing the nasty grin of a killer.

"We already know how this ends, young siren," she giggled. "Don't make me do something I could soon regret."

She then gave a pout and quivered her lip.

Strike stood there without a struggle. He looked into Jace's dark brown eyes and nodded before grabbing her hand and twisting the knife as it left a gap in his throat. She then yelled and threw him to the ground. Angel quickly vanished, and Jace and Brad rushed over feeling his neck.

All of the blood poured onto the ground. Strike

had no breath left to even speak. Jace had to close his eyes, letting him rest in peace.

"Everything leads to my time," Jace whispered. "I just wish nobody would die because of me."

"Jace, you can't save everyone."

Scarlett placed her hand on his shoulder. Brad rolled his eyes and huffed under his breath.

CHAPTER 17
CHRONIC: THE ALL-BEING

Drago stood out on the terrace that overlooked the great city of Atlas. CyberTek was located in the center of the beautiful city and was the only major building, even after having been abandoned so long ago.

He then heard Angel groaning and moaning before planting herself in a chair. He turned with a smile on his face as he walked back inside.

"So, Krater was able to help the kid control the power." He smiled.

Angel smiled and nodded her head quickly trying to allow her bruises to heal up. She then saw a bright blue light enter the room. A man who was in a long dark robe that was made from chrome material. Or at least to Angel's blind eyes, it seemed that way.

"Chronic," Drago whispered. "The stories are true."

Chronic smiled. "Bringing Blackheart back will not change what is coming."

He walked around him, the bottom of his robe dragging across the ground.

Drago kept his attention on him, circling him.

"I am starting to learn about this so-called 'siren warrior.' So far, he is stronger than even Krater, almighty."

"So that is how Krater managed to come back from the hole he was in," Drago chuckled.

Chronic snickered and stared outside the thirty-story window of Cybertek.

"Has he tried to surpass you yet?"

Drago stopped for a moment, clenched his fists, and gave a sharp growl.

"Nobody is capable of taking me down so easily. What could make you so sure?"

Chronic laughed, "I am the all-being. I know everything that is to come."

His voice then echoed as he vanished into the air. The robe dropped to the floor, and Drago was left with too many questions. His ego, though, hid his intentions to care.

"Make sure that Blackheart is ready to be resurrected," he told Angel. "Not much longer, and the boy will reach the final peak of his siren power, and I must be ready for the final step."

"What does that mean for you, though?" she asked.

Drago sighed and smiled. "I may not be here when the dark lord returns. If Chronic is right about this and the siren warrior is stronger than I am, then it was an accomplishment in the end."

Drago then jumped out the window and landed on the ground. Angel then saw the black stone starting to crack. She gave a slight grin and stored the stone inside a capsule with the machine still running, and the lights beamed through, lighting up the entire building. She could hear a sudden buzzing sound, and the machine started to turn clockwise constantly.

With a smirk, she then whispered, "All hail Blackheart."

CHAPTER 18

LEVELING THE PLAYING FIELD

J ace swung his sword across Scarlett as she dodged quickly. He could feel the sweat streaming down, covering his entire face. Scarlett suggested a break, but he insisted on keeping going.

"The anger is not going to go away, Jace." She told him. "Please just call it and rest."

Jace shook his head. "I must end this. I have put a lot of people through pain and death already, and after everything, I don't want to go through this. I am giving up."

"That is not going to be so easy," she sighed.

Scarlett felt him swing his sword again, and she blocked it, knocking it out of his hand then held the blade against his neck as he fell to his knees. Jace released a nervous laugh and stood up.

"Kade is missing, Scarlett," Jace reminded her. "We could be out there trying to find him. It is the same scenario as my decision to step away from becoming some 'hero.'"

Scarlett stood silent. She threw the blade down and grabbed Jace by the arm, throwing him over her shoulder to the ground. She then sat on one knee with her finger pointed directly at his nose. He felt the pointy end of her fingernail poking, shedding a pinch of blood.

"My search for my brother and your need to run and hide are most certainly not the same. April, Ty, and Jonathan risked their lives protecting you and I think they were heroes at that point." She then stood up and left Jace alone.

Maybe she was right. Jace knew it deep down. He just wanted his life to be back to normal and not to be afraid that somebody would die in his name or just to protect who he was.

Jace stood outside Castle Oblivion with a bottle of water in his hand gargling it down. Brad then stood next to him with a beer in his hand. Jace scoffed.

"It's a little early for that, isn't it?" he asked with a chuckle.

Brad mocked him.

"It is never too early for a cold drink," he replied.

Jace smiled. "Have you found where Kade may have gone?"

Brad shook his head and sighed deeply. He told him that it was as if he had fallen off the grid and was just gone—lost.

Scarlett then cleared her throat.

"There is something you two need to come see."

The two then followed her down to the shores of the island. The clouds were turning into blackness and thunder, with cracks of lightning swarming around them as if a storm were coming, but with no rain falling.

"It is beginning," Scarlett mentioned. "The awakening. Blackheart will be resurrected soon, and there is no sign of Drago."

"That's what he wants," Jace told her.

"What?" She raised a brow.

Jace turned his head. "Drago is sending that as a message. He wants me, and somehow something is happening; I just can't figure out what."

"A trip back home?" Brad asked.

Scarlett then looked up at the castle, and with a sigh, she shook her head.

"You both go on. Finding Kade is my only priority, and I may have a location. Just don't get yourselves killed."

She then headed back up to the castle, and the boys packed up quickly before leaving the Isles. Jace slouched in his chair, and Brad sat quietly in the pilot's seat, soaring through the clouds even though it was completely dark and foggy. It was almost hard for them to see where they were or if they were close to a mountain high enough to crash into.

"She will be all right," Brad assured him.

"I know," Jace sighed. "I just can't shake the feeling that something is happening beyond just Drago."

The clouds began to break apart and they flew over Bright Burn City, Jace's hometown. He could still feel the dark energy that was left and forgotten after the death of his aunt and the damage that was created.

He told Brad to land on a steep hill where they could be hidden from the city and the people who might poke their noses outside the city limits. Jace stood outside and smelled the fresh stench of industrial takeover and burning smoke.

It smelled like home.

"Be cautious, Jace," Brad advised him. "You haven't been here for a long time, and we have to watch out for anything."

Jace nodded. He then headed into the heart of town, where the street led from a shop called "The Quad" that sold old comic books to a graveyard where his mother and aunt were buried. He stood over the tombstones, reading their names aloud before shedding a tear.

"You swore you would never allow me to go through this life and let me just be normal." He thought to himself. "This is just not me. I never asked for this. I have lost Ty and now it is only a matter of time what could happen next."

He then heard a woman mention him talking out loud to himself, startling him as he quickly jumped up to see Jackie standing there with a smile.

"Gone for months, and I had a feeling someday you would be here again," she smiled.

Jace sighed. "I thought coming here would make me less afraid."

"Always have to be stubborn," she laughed.

Jace smiled and rolled his eyes to look at the tombstones.

"Did you know I would be here?"

"Honestly," she stood next to him, staring down, "there were many times when I was waiting for you to come knocking on your best friend's window. Not at a cemetery. I have been here many times, just hoping I could see my best friend once more. I can tell that you had it rough, though."

She smiled, patted his arm, then sat on a bench a few feet away from the graveyard.

Jace followed her down with his arms folded.

There was thunder rumbling loudly, hidden in the clouds, and an occasional lightning bolt lit up the night sky.

"The sun vanished just earlier today." Jackie looked up.

Jace sighed. "This is my last chance to end this. I just can't be who I am destined to be."

Jackie hummed. "So, it is true. The dark skies and the sudden thunder and lightning. It's finally happening."

Jace chuckled as his palms started to glow a bright blue and flames covered his eyes. The clouds began to clear just slightly, as if they were frightened of what he could do and he would kill them in an instant. Jackie's eyes lit up, and she could see flames dancing through the clouds, creating energy that not many could see.

It was like a metaphor.

Jace looked up and saw Drago walking slowly

with a grin and a shadow walker by his side. Limping, his long arms hung down to the ground. Sharp teeth were as sharp as toothpicks.

"If this is it, you can do anything you put your mind to. That is the best friend that I know."

Jackie then kissed his cheek, and she was gone.

It was as if she was never even there, and the only one who was truly there was Drago. Jace kept looking around but saw Drago stop in front of him.

"What are you searching for?" Drago scoffed.

"That had to be in my mind," Jace whispered. "I know why you are here, Drago."

Drago then smiled, and the shadow walker rushed after Jace, knocking him down, with his long, snake-like tongue close to Jace's face. His eyes burst into flames, and as the shadow walker was locked onto Jace, even with his energy becoming stronger, the monster was stronger.

Drago laughed. "I continue to question how someone such as Krater could fall to a child who does not even come close to understanding what being a siren truly is. But then I think to myself, 'Even Krater had his weakest points.' Color me intrigued."

CHAPTER 19

SEARCHING FOR THE TRUTH

Scarlett stopped outside Ryker's Castle, not too far from the Kingdom of Legion, where she found the last contact who could be her only hope in finding Kade. She walked up the 10,000 steps that led straight upward toward a darkened castle gateway. She could hear the echoes of the past, where her father, King Leo, had set foot on those steps.

It was crazy to see the castle after all the years, and Lord Ryker was not going to be pleased to see the daughter of a king who abandoned the land because of his ego. But she grabbed the handle and heard the ringing of bells as she slammed it against the door three times before the giant wooden doors opened.

Ryker gave a grumbling growl when he saw her. Scarlett stood there, firm and quiet.

"Princess Scarlett," he said with a sneer. "Isn't this a strange surprise?"

Scarlett rolled her eyes and followed Ryker to the throne room. She hesitated as she told him that there was something they needed to discuss. She knew how it was going to go, and with the right offer, she knew this was her only shot.

"Kade has been missing since yesterday," she began. "Angelina was with him last, and when I returned inside the castle after their confrontation, he was gone. You are the only one who might know what happened and where he may be."

Ryker then laughed hysterically.

"The Prince of Kingdom Legion has disappeared? Leonardo truly left his kingdom in the wrong hands."

"Look," Scarlett shouted, "our family feud has been going on long enough. I lost my best friend over a stupid decision and final last words. I am not going to lose my brother after the horrible things I said to him."

Ryker gave a smile and told her about a man named Von Dar, an all-being who could destroy an entire world. He was once a human in medieval times until one day he turned against the world by creating a machine that no mortal could ever think of at the time. Technology wasn't exactly existent at the time.

"He may have been the one who took your brother. Von was always hired by Dark Angel, even when your father and mother were still alive. He was tried when your father was a child, and he looked up to him. If you wish to find your brother, he is the only one who could have possibly done it."

Scarlett groaned. "If Von was locked away, how could he possibly have Kade?"

Ryker sighed, and a crystal ball sat on a stand. He told her to look within the crystal. She could see Kade standing there with Angelina across from him while the battle was going on, and a giant form of fog surrounded the room. A man stood there after the fog dissipated, wearing a long cloak. Kade tried charging after him, but the man grabbed him by the neck, lifting him into the air, and quickly vanished.

Leaving the crystal to turn black.

Scarlett stumbled, and she felt her heart drop. She had never seen a man form some kind of cloud of fog just like that and vanish afterward. It was almost impossible.

"If finding your brother is what you truly want, then take the road that leads to the darkest corridors," Ryker told her.

She then saw a door open, and a dark road appeared. She was not sure where it would take her or what he exactly meant by "the darkest corridors."

Kade was her only priority.

CHAPTER 20

FALLEN

J ace stood there, waiting for Drago to make a move. Jace knew that Drago was holding back and wanted him to charge first. With the anger and the need to end Drago's crusade that Jace held in, Drago knew.

"You killed Ty," Jace growled and clenched his fists. "My whole family has died at your hands, and you have no remorse, Drago."

His eyes then filled the area with blue flames burning bright, and he leaped up. Drago looked up and smiled as Jace swooped down without a thought. Drago could feel the anger in his punches, but it fueled Drago. He wanted this.

Drago then grabbed his fist tightly and threw him back. Jace crashed through the tombstones across the cemetery, and Drago huffed, not feeling a pinch of sweat on his white skin. He didn't even need to kick his foot back to quickly appear over Jace. It was like he was a ghost in the moonlight and a shadow appearing out of nowhere, just seeing black smoke beneath his feet.

Drago lifted Jace from the ground, giving a grinning smile as he watched Jace struggle.

"You are a siren. You must know how to fight by now, hm?"

He chuckled and threw Jace down like a ragdoll. Jace could still feel the energy pulsing through him, but it didn't seem enough.

"Your mother and father must be so disappointed in you."

Jace then groaned, and Drago held his tall boot against Jace's chest, making it hard for him to get back up.

Jace hated hearing his parents even being mentioned in the man's breath who started it all. Jace then took an angry breath and leaped after Drago without a thought, dragging him across the ground.

You could see the look in Drago's eyes: fear.

Something that he had never experienced before, and this was a first. Jace stood over Drago and grabbed him by the neck once more. Drago could feel the flames warming the skin that was inside Jace's eyes, just burning the flesh. That's what it felt like to him anyway.

"Keep my family out of your mouth,"

He growled and swung his fist upward, causing Drago's body to free-fall through the air, slamming into the ground.

Drago tried dragging himself up to his feet, only to fall over and over again. Jace quickly rushed in, standing over Drago with that fierce vengeance in his core. He was filled with hatred, and his conscience was clouded with judgment.

He wanted to kill the man, but for what?

He took his family already. Krater killed April and Drago had plenty to do with his father's disappearance, as well as his mother's illness destroying her lungs. He could only begin to blame his mother's death on Drago.

Jace then felt a ball of energy forming in his palm. The ball was so close it felt like it was touching his body while being so far away from him. Drago tried begging, but no words would come out. Jace was never given the time to do so.

Jace then felt someone grab his arm. It was as if time stopped, and Drago was frozen in time. There was no breeze blowing the trees around him, and no chirping from the birds above.

He turned his head to a ghost. Or a spirit that wore the same face as his mother. It was strange, but it was as if he could feel his mother's touch, and it felt so real.

But how could it be? That was the one question that haunted his mind right then and there.

"Mom,"

he whispered, and she smiled as she laid his arm down, allowing the ball of energy to deplete.

"This isn't you, Jace." She smiled.

"He is the reason why I lost so many,"

Jace sobbed and turned his head to Drago's frozen face.

"He doesn't deserve to live."

Ashley then turned his attention back to her, giving her a warm smile, and said,

"His soul must be trapped. It is not punishment for those who deserve it, even if it seems that way. You are better than this, my son, and you are a light-bringer. You have kindness out of the sirens before you. You must let go. Let go of the tears and the fear of trying. Reach for your heart and be free."

Her voice then echoed, and she was gone.

Time then rolled back, and Drago was still sitting there, begging for his life. Jace took a deep breath and locked onto Drago's wrist with his eyes closed and all Drago could feel was his soul turning black, and he saw a white light flashing before losing his breath.

Jace sighed with relief. He fell to the ground, and he could hear footsteps approaching. Brad stood over him, and Scarlett wasn't too far behind. Brad stared up at the black skies. The lightning flashed in the sky, causing the entire night to light up every five seconds.

"It is getting worse," Scarlett said.

Jace smiled. "We lost so much."

He stood up and began to walk away.

"It wasn't your fault, Jace," Scarlett shouted. "You can't give up."

Jace said nothing. He vanished and Brad scoffed under his breath. Scarlett rolled her eyes and with the classical, 'shut up' remarks they both stood there.

"Maybe it is good that he is giving up," Brad said bluntly.

"You don't mean that," Scarlett assured him.

Brad was silent and he walked away. Scarlett looked down at April and Ashley's tombstones, giving a deep sigh before leaving.

The End.

www.ingramcontent.com/pod-product-compliance
Lightning Source LLC
Chambersburg PA
CBHW060932140726
47996CB00001B/466